W9-AQV-053

to Jack, Harry and Ella

www.JadeTreeBooks.com

Copyright © 2014 by Lilly Waters
Printed in China
Published, 2014 Philadelphia, PA
ISBN 978-0-9888610-0-8
Library of Congress Control Number: 2014935624

Hurry Harry! Hurry!

by Lilly Waters

illustrated by
Valerie Quinn

Jade Tree Books LLC

Hurry Harry! Hur

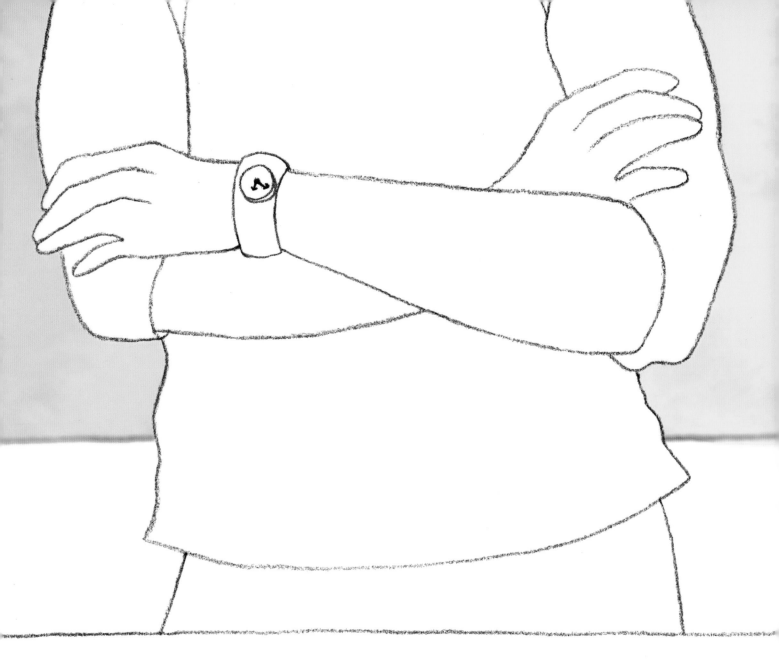

Hurry Harry! Hurry!

Hurry Harry!

Hurry!

Hurry Harry! Hurry! Hurry!

Hurry Harry! Hurry!

Wow Harry! Wow!

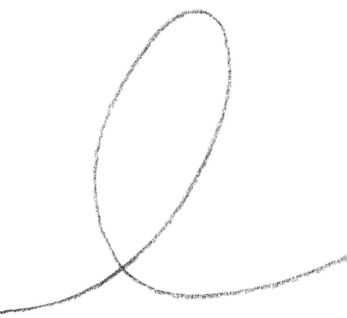